Mae
the Panda
Fairy

by Daisy Meadows

ORCHARD

www.rainbowmagic.co.uk

The Fairyland Palace

Meadow

Stream

Beehive

Arctic Tundra

Eucalyptus Forest

Tropical Waterfall

Wild Woods
Nature
Reserve

Watering Hole

Pagoda

Jack Frost's
Ice Castle

To Jack Frost's Zoo ↱

Desert Oasis

Jack Frost's Spell

I love animals, yes I do,
I want my very own private zoo!
I'll capture the animals one by one,
With fairy magic to help me on!

A koala, a tiger, an Arctic fox,
I'll keep them in cages with giant locks.
Every kind of animal will be there,
A panda, a meerkat, a honey bear.
The animals will be my property,
I'll be master of a huge menagerie!

Contents

A Visitor from Fairyland

Kirsty Tate gazed happily at the tall hedgerows, her bare arm resting on the open window as the car travelled along the bumpy country road. Pretty red, yellow and pink flowers were tangled among the green leaves. She could smell the tang of cut grass and the earthiness of freshly turned soil.

"We're nearly there, girls," said Mrs Tate from the driver's seat. "Look!"

She slowed the car and pointed at a signpost at the side of the winding road. **WILD WOODS NATURE RESERVE – 2 MILES**

Kirsty smiled at her best friend Rachel Walker, who was sitting beside her.

"I'm so excited," said Rachel. "The sun's shining, we've got all of the summer holidays stretched out ahead of us, and a whole week to spend here at the reserve with the animals."

It was the start of the summer holidays, and Kirsty and Rachel were on their way to Wild Woods, their local nature reserve. Rachel was staying with Kirsty, and their parents had arranged for them to spend every day that week there as volunteers. As the car turned up a rough, narrow track, their hearts were racing with anticipation.

"It's going to be amazing to be helping out as junior rangers," said Kirsty. "I can't wait to see the animals!"

At the end of the track was an archway, printed with green words:

WELCOME TO WILD WOODS
NATURE RESERVE

Mrs Tate drove through the archway and stopped the car next to a small wooden hut. The door of the hut opened and a tanned, dark-haired woman came out. She was wearing khaki shorts, a white shirt and walking boots, and she waved at them with a smile.

"Look, there's Becky," said Mrs Tate. "She's the head of Wild Woods."

Rachel and Kirsty jumped out of the car and Becky walked over to them.

"It's great to meet you both," said Becky, shaking their hands. "I'm really pleased that you're going to be spending this week with us. It's great to meet young people who are interested in conservation."

"We can't wait to get started!" said Rachel excitedly.

"I thought you should begin by going off on your own to explore the reserve," said Becky. "It's the best way to get a feel for it. I'll meet you back here this afternoon and give you your first task."

"That sounds like great fun!" Kirsty cheered.

"A real adventure!" Rachel added.

"These two love adventures!" said Mrs Tate with a laugh.

The girls exchanged a secret, happy glance. Kirsty's mother had no idea how many adventures they had already had!

They were friends with all the Rainbow Magic fairies, and had often visited Fairyland and helped foil Jack Frost's spiteful plans.

They grabbed their backpacks and put on their hats.

"Have you got everything?" asked Mrs Tate kindly.

Kirsty peered into her backpack.

"Camera, notebook, waterproofs, pens, binoculars, plasters..." She grinned at her mother. "Yes, I think I've remembered everything!"

Mrs Tate kissed her and gave Kirsty a hug. "Have a fantastic time," she said.

Rachel and Kirsty waved goodbye and hurried down a winding path into the reserve. As soon as they were out of sight, Kirsty paused and took a deep breath of

fresh air. "I feel as if there's no one else around for miles and miles," she said.

"It's wonderful!" Rachel smiled, turning around slowly on the spot.

"I can see dragonflies, bumble bees and even a kingfisher!"

They were standing beside a large pond, which was surrounded by tall rushes. Everywhere they looked, they saw animals. Hares peeped out at them, ducks paddled in the shallows and otters slipped into the water. Kirsty fumbled in

her backpack and pulled out her camera.

"This place is incredible," she said, taking picture after picture.

"Look over there," said Rachel, pulling out her camera too. "The frog on that lily pad looks just like my green frog toy at home."

"He does look familiar," Kirsty agreed, looking through her camera lens and zooming in. "Hang on – that's no ordinary frog! It's Bertram!" Their friend the Royal Frog Footman from Fairyland waved and came hopping over to them.

Rachel and Kirsty knelt down beside the edge of the pond and smiled at him.

"Hello, Rachel and Kirsty!" he said in a surprised voice. "I didn't expect to meet you two here!"

"We didn't expect to see you either," said Rachel with a giggle.

"I have relatives in the human world," Bertram explained. "I've just been to visit them."

"We're here helping out at the nature

reserve," Kirsty explained. "We're having a look around."

"Yes, this is quite a good nature reserve," said Bertram. "Not as good as the one in Fairyland, of course."

"I didn't know there was a nature reserve in Fairyland," said Rachel.

"Oh yes, it's wonderful there," said Bertram. "Would you like to visit?"

"Yes, please!" said Rachel.

"We'd love to!" Kirsty exclaimed. "But how can we get there without fairy magic?"

"Should we use our lockets?" asked Rachel. "They've got a little bit of fairy dust inside them."

"There's no need for that," said Bertram with a smile. "We animals have a little magic of our own!"

Animal Thief!

There was a far-off sound like leaves rustling in the wind, and then a silvery starburst surrounded them. The girls felt wings growing on their backs as they shrank to fairy-size. When the sparkles cleared, they were standing in a fairy glade beside Bertram.

They heard a cry of surprise and saw their old friend Fluffy the Squirrel staring up at them in astonishment.

"Rachel! Kirsty!" he exclaimed. "Welcome to the Fairyland Nature Reserve! I didn't know you were visiting Fairyland today."

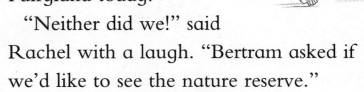

"Neither did we!" said Rachel with a laugh. "Bertram asked if we'd like to see the nature reserve."

"You're always welcome here," said Fluffy. "Follow me and I'll give you a guided tour."

The girls said goodbye to Bertram and then set off after Fluffy. He scampered off down a winding path, and moments

later they were flying through a snowy
Antarctic scene, surrounded by penguins.
Kirsty and Rachel still had their cameras
around their necks, and they snapped
photo after photo of the beautiful
black-and-white animals.

Around the next corner was a jungle habitat. Fluffy leapt through the high trees, calling out to the cheeky monkeys who were swinging from the branches. *Snap! Snap! Snap!* Rachel and Kirsty's cameras were filling up with photos.

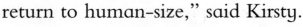

"I wonder if these photos will come out all right when the cameras return to human-size," said Kirsty.

"If they do, let's promise to keep them a secret," said Rachel.

Fluffy paused to talk to a red-and-gold parrot, and the girls landed on a branch and linked their little fingers in the special best friends promise. Then they shared a happy smile. They hadn't expected their nature reserve trip to be this exciting!

Fluffy scampered down a tree and into a spring meadow, filled with buttercups and daisies. Rachel and Kirsty followed.

"It's wonderful how we can travel from one habitat to another so fast," said Kirsty happily.

On the far side of the meadow was a fluttering cloud of butterflies. Rachel pointed them out in delight and lifted her camera to take a picture.

"They're coming this way," she said.

"Hang on," said Kirsty. "They're much too big to be butterflies. They're fairies!"

The girls started waving, and the seven pretty fairies flew towards them, smiling in excitement.

"You're Rachel and Kirsty, aren't you?" asked a dark-haired fairy with a pretty patterned top. "We weren't expecting such important visitors today! We're the Baby Animal Rescue Fairies and we look after all the baby animals in the Fairyland Nature Reserve. I'm Kimberley the Koala Fairy."

"It's lovely to meet you," said Rachel with a beaming smile.

The other fairies introduced themselves as Kitty the Tiger Fairy, Mara the Meerkat Fairy, Savannah the Zebra Fairy, Mae the Panda Fairy, Rosie the Honey Bear Fairy and Anna the Arctic Fox Fairy. The girls noticed that each fairy had an animal key ring clipped to her clothes, to match the animal she looked after.

"I hope you don't mind us taking a few photos?" asked Kirsty.

"Of course not," said Kimberley. "I hope you get some good pictures. All the animals are friendly, as long as you don't get too close or startle them."

Suddenly there was a gigantic roar and the ground started to shake. The fairies clutched at one another in fear.

"What is it?" cried Anna.

"An earthquake!" Savannah exclaimed.

They saw Bertram hopping towards them, shouting and waving. The noise grew even louder and, all around the meadow, birds flew into the air, petrified. Terrified woodland animals raced this way and that in the grass, not knowing which direction to choose. The girls turned around and gasped. An enormous ice-blue monster truck was hurtling towards them at fast speed!

The truck screeched to a halt inches from where they were standing. The engine was turned off and the roar stopped. Then Jack Frost opened the door and jumped out, followed by several goblins. Bertram arrived beside the girls, looking very cross.

"Your stupid truck has scared all the animals!" he cried.

"Nonsense, frog face," snapped Jack Frost. "I LOVE animals! That's why I'm here! I want one of every kind of animal in the world for my own personal zoo."

"But that's wrong," said Rachel. "Animals are living creatures, not objects to be collected."

"Rubbish!" Jack Frost hissed. "Anyway, it's none of your business."

"Well, it's definitely *our* business,"

said Mara, stepping forward. "We're
the Baby Animal Rescue Fairies. If you
won't listen to our friends, perhaps you'll
listen to us."

"Fat chance!" cackled one of the
goblins, standing behind Jack Frost.

"Yah boo, sucks to you," said another
goblin rudely, putting his thumb to his
nose and waggling his fingers.

Jack Frost just curled his lip
and lifted his wand.

"You'll never stop
My selfish joys!
You silly fairies,
I'll take your toys!"

He waved his wand and there was
a blinding bolt of icy-blue magic. In a
flash, Jack Frost was holding all seven of
the fairies' animal key rings!

Lost!

The fairies cried out and Jack Frost laughed, throwing the toys into the air and juggling with them.

"Give those back!" Rachel demanded.

"What, these?" asked Jack Frost, holding them out to her.

Rachel reached out to take them, and he snatched them away, cackling with laughter. He threw them to his goblins, who dropped them all.

"BUTTERFINGERS!" Jack Frost roared. "Pick them up NOW, and round up every animal in this crummy nature reserve. I'll take them all!"

"Yes sir, right away sir!" babbled the goblins, gathering the toys into their arms.

"We have to stop them!" Kirsty exclaimed, looking worried.

Fluffy leapt forward and squeaked at

the goblins as loudly as he could. The
cowardly goblins screamed and ran
away, still clutching the key rings. Jack
Frost watched them disappear among
the distant trees, and shook his fist after
them. Then he turned to face the fairies.
His eyes narrowed to
mean slits.

"Fine," he said.
"FINE! If I can't
have these Fairyland
animals, I'll just take
animals from the
human world instead!"

He jumped back into
his truck and it roared into life. A huge
cloud of blue smoke puffed into the
fairies' faces. Then the truck zoomed
away and disappeared from sight.

"What are we going to do?" asked
Rosie. "Without our magical key rings,
we can't protect the animals in the
human world!"

Kitty turned to Rachel and Kirsty with
tears in her eyes.

"We have to stop him and save the
animals," she said. "But how?"

"We'll help," said Rachel at once.

"We'll do everything we can," said
Kirsty. "I don't know where we're going
to start, though."

Mae the Panda Fairy threw her arms
around the girls.

"Thank you so
much," she said.
"The other
fairies have
told us how kind

you are. And I think I have an idea that might help."

She whispered something to the six other Baby Animal Rescue Fairies, and then they all lifted their wands together and waved them in unison. Coloured fairy dust swirled from the tips of their wands and coiled together in the air, forming a small sparkling cloud. It moved over the heads of Rachel and Kirsty, and then sprinkled down on them.

Instantly, the noises around them seemed to change. The air had been full of the squawks of birds, but now the squawks sounded more like voices. Adding to the noise, there were soft, squeaky voices from below their feet.

"Where's my nest? I've lost my nest!"

"Whose feet are these?"

"What's that? Is it food?"

"Who said that?" asked Rachel in amazement.

The fairies laughed.

"We've just given you the ability to understand animals," said Mae. "It should help you to find our magic key rings."

Rachel and Kirsty shared a thrilled smile, holding hands.

"I want to visit my panda friends in the human world," said Mae. "I must warn them that Jack Frost might be coming. Will you come with me?"

Rachel and Kirsty nodded eagerly, and Mae lifted her wand above her head.

"Let Rachel and Kirsty come and see
Where pandas wander wild and free."

Instantly, the meadow around the girls vanished. They were standing beside a beautiful pagoda at the top of a mountain, and they were human-sized again. A dense forest of bamboo covered the mountain. Mae was fluttering beside them, looking around in delight. It was obvious that she loved this place.

Even though it was warm, it was also raining. The girls pulled their waterproofs out of their bags and put them on. Mae tucked herself inside Rachel's hood.

"Come on, let's go," she said. "Keep a look out for the pandas!"

They pushed their way between the tall bamboo stems, and raindrops pattered down on their hoods.

They hadn't gone very far before Kirsty heard a rustling sound. She reached out her hand and held Rachel's arm.

"Listen!" she whispered.

Rachel suddenly felt as if it were Christmas Eve and Santa was on his way. Could they really be about to see a real-life panda in the wild? They crept towards the sound, treading as softly as they could. Then they heard a soft voice calling through the forest.

"Pan Pan, where are you?"

"Who's that?" asked Rachel to Mae in a low voice.

The voice was sad and urgent. "Come back to Mama," it said again.

Then Kirsty spotted a giant panda in a tree above them.

"We can understand animals now," she said. "Remember the fairies' spell?"

"Of course!' said Rachel. "Wow!"

Kirsty waved at the beautiful panda.

"Hello," she called. "I'm Kirsty and this

is my friend Rachel."

The giant panda's eyes
widened, but she didn't
reply. She just stared
down at them, looking
confused and scared.

Mae flew out of
Kirsty's hood and zoomed
up to hover beside the giant panda.
The girls couldn't hear what she was
saying, but after a long pause, the panda
began to climb down the tree. She
moved quickly and gracefully. When she
reached the ground, she turned and sat
down beside the girls.

"I'm sorry I didn't answer you at first,"
she said. "I didn't know if I could trust
you. My baby, my little Pan Pan, has
disappeared!"

The Bamboo Forest

"I'm so sorry," said Rachel, putting her hand on Mother Panda's paw. "Will you tell us about it? We might be able to help you."

"Pan Pan is only seven months old," said Mother Panda. "He's just started eating bamboo, so I went to find him some extra-juicy shoots. When I came back, he was gone!"

Rachel and Kirsty exchanged a suspicious glance.

"Do you think that the goblins might have taken Pan Pan for Jack Frost?" asked Kirsty.

"We need to see exactly where you last saw Pan Pan," said Rachel to Mother Panda. "Can you take us there?"

Mother Panda led them deeper into the bamboo forest, until they reached a big clearing.

"This is where I last saw Pan Pan," she said sadly.

Rachel and Kirsty looked around, and then Rachel gave a shout.

"Over there. Look!" she cried.

They could see huge footprints in the mud. Whoever had made them had toes that splayed wide and large, flat feet.

"Goblins!" said Kirsty. "I knew it! I bet that if we follow these footprints, we'll find Pan Pan."

"It'll be easier to follow them if we can all fly," said Mae. She flicked her wand, and there was a small explosion of silver fairy dust that made Mother Panda jump. The silver sparkles swirled around the two girls, and as they shrank to fairy-size they felt their wings growing on their backs.

"We'll be back as soon as we have news of Pan Pan," Kirsty promised Mother Panda.

The three fairies rose into the air and waved goodbye to Mother Panda. Then they followed the huge footprints away from the clearing and through the forest of bamboo.

"Bamboo trees are amazingly tall," said Rachel. "I didn't know they could grow so high."

"Bamboo is one of the fastest-growing plants in the world," Mae told them in a proud voice. "It makes a wonderful food for pandas."

"I hope it stays like this for ever," said Kirsty to Mae.

They hadn't been following the footprints for very long before they heard a lot of shrieking and squawking.

"That sounds like goblins," said Rachel. "Come on!"

They zigzagged through the trees
and bamboo stems until they reached a
babbling mountain stream. There, on the
bank, were four noisy goblins!

Three of the goblins seemed to be
trying to push each other into the water.
The fourth goblin, who had very large
ears, was sitting on a log cuddling
something black-and-white in his arms.

"It's Pan Pan!" cried Mae.

The fairies fluttered closer and hid behind some bamboo leaves. The goblin was tickling Pan Pan with a little fluffy toy, and the panda was chuckling.

"Mae, that's your magical key ring, isn't it?" asked Kirsty in excitement.

Mae nodded eagerly. "You're right. Oh girls, we've found the baby panda

and my key ring. But how can we get them both back from the goblin?"

Just then, the three goblins who had been squabbling on the bank turned to the goblin with big ears.

"We've been messing around here long enough," said the tallest goblin. "Stop cuddling that panda. We have to get it to the Ice Castle to be the first animal in Jack Frost's zoo."

"Not IT, HIM!" shouted the big-eared goblin. "Anyway, we can't go yet. He's very thirsty!"

The other three goblins rolled their eyes as he stood up and took Pan Pan over to the clear stream. He put the little panda down to have a few sips of water. When Pan Pan had had enough, he sat back and looked around. The big-eared goblin held out the magical toy, and Pan Pan scampered back to him and snuggled up in his lap.

"Right," said the tallest goblin. "Now let's go."

"We can't go just yet," said the big-eared goblin. "He's having a snooze."

The other goblins groaned and Kirsty turned to Mae with a frown.

"Why does Pan Pan like the goblin so much?" she asked.

"It's my magic," said Mae sadly. "Animals are attracted to my key ring. It helps them to trust me when I first meet them."

Rachel's eyes opened very wide.

"Of course!" she said. "That's how the goblins kidnapped Pan Pan."

"So we have to get the key ring back before we can rescue him," said Kirsty. "I have an idea. Mae, can you turn me into a goblin?"

"All right," said Mae, sounding a little nervous. "Get ready!"

She raised her wand and Kirsty closed her eyes. She didn't like turning into a goblin. But she would do anything to help return Pan Pan to his mother.

A Daring Rescue

Kirsty felt her nose growing longer and her ears becoming pointed as her hair disappeared. Holding out her hands in front of her, she saw that they had gone green. Mae and Rachel, who were fluttering in the air beside her, suddenly looked very small.

"Wish me luck!" said Kirsty.

"Good luck!" whispered Mae and Rachel together.

Kirsty stepped out from behind the thicket of bamboo, and sat down beside the goblin with the big ears.

"Hello," she said, making her voice sound as squawky as she could. "Would you like me to hold that toy while you rock the panda to sleep?"

"Don't be stupid," said the goblin rudely. "This toy's the only thing keeping the panda with me. If you took the toy, he'd go to you instead."

"I didn't know that!" screeched a plump goblin.

He snatched the magical key ring and Pan Pan woke up with a jump. Instantly, the little panda scampered after his toy. But another goblin grabbed it, and Pan Pan changed direction. With a cry of fury, the goblin with the big ears hurled

himself after the others and seized the
key ring.

Kirsty leapt up and chased the big-
eared goblin, trying to snatch the
magical key ring out of his hands.
But then she heard a whimpering noise.
Poor little Pan Pan was crying. He didn't
understand what was happening –
he just wanted his toy back.

Mae couldn't bear to see him crying.

"We have to stop this!" she said.

She flew out from her hiding place, closely followed by Rachel.

"FAIRIES!" screeched the tallest goblins. "Get them! Trap them!"

Rachel zoomed towards the big-eared goblin, and Kirsty started jumping up and down.

"There's a fairy right behind you!" she yelled at the goblin. "Quick, throw the toy to me!"

The goblin hurled the key ring to Kirsty. Instantly, Pan Pan toddled over to her. She scooped him up in her arms and gave Rachel and Mae a beaming smile.

"We did it!" she said as they landed on her shoulders. "Pan Pan is safe."

"And so is my key ring," said Mae, her

eyes sparkling with happiness.

Kirsty handed her the toy, and it shrank to fairy-size. Pan Pan gave a sad squeak as Mae clipped it to her belt. Rachel fluttered down and stroked Pan Pan's wet little nose.

"Don't be sad," she said in a soft voice. "We're taking you home to your mother."

The goblins were gaping at Kirsty in amazement. They still thought that she was one of them!

"What did you do that for?" bawled the tallest goblin. "Are you off your rocker? Jack Frost will be furious!"

Mae waved her wand, and Kirsty was transformed into a human again. The goblins let out howls of rage.

"You rotten, tricksy fairies!"

"Cheats! Cheats!"

"Give that panda back!"

The tallest goblin turned to the goblin with big ears and stamped on his foot.

"This is all your fault!" he squawked. "If we'd gone when I said we should, we'd be at the Ice Castle by now!"

"What's Jack Frost going to say?" asked the plump goblin, his knees knocking together.

"Maybe we should go into hiding," said the fourth goblin.

"Good idea!" said the tallest goblin. "Come on, let's run for it!"

The girls and Pan Pan watched as the goblins disappeared into the bamboo forest. Then Mae returned Rachel to human-size.

"May I have a cuddle with Pan Pan?" Rachel asked at once.

Kirsty smiled and handed her the little panda. Just then, they heard running footsteps and the goblin with big ears came hurrying back out of the bamboo forest. Rachel held on tightly to Pan Pan. What was the goblin going to do?

A Panda Present

The goblin stopped in front of Rachel and looked embarrassed.

"I just wanted to say goodbye," he said in a shy voice.

Rachel bent down and let him give Pan Pan a tickle.

"Goodbye, little panda," he whispered.

Then he scurried away, and Rachel lifted Pan Pan onto her shoulders.

"Pan Pan, you're so sweet that you even melted the heart of a goblin," said Kirsty with a laugh. "Come on, let's take you home."

Together, the girls and Mae made their way back through the crackling bamboo stems and the wet grass. They found Mother Panda sheltering under the beautiful pagoda.

As soon as she saw them, Mother
Panda gave a happy cry.

"Pan Pan!"

With a squeal of delight, Pan Pan
jumped off Rachel's shoulders and ran
into his mother's arms. As she showered
him in furry, snuffly kisses, she looked at
the girls with tears in her eyes.

"How can I ever thank you?" she
asked happily.

"There is one thing," said Kirsty with a little smile. "Would you let us take a picture of you and Pan Pan?"

A few minutes later, Rachel and Kirsty had some beautiful shots of Pan Pan and his mother.

"Now it's time for us to go home," said Rachel, looking at her watch. "We've got to meet Becky at the nature reserve!"

Mae gave each of the girls a butterfly kiss on the cheek.

"You've been wonderful," she said. "I couldn't have saved Pan Pan or my magical key ring without you. Thank you!"

"You're welcome," said Kirsty. "The
Baby Animal Rescue Fairies can always
count on our help."

"We're going to need it," said Mae.
"There are still six magical key rings to
find. But in the meantime, I'll send you
back to Wild Woods Nature Reserve.
Goodbye, girls!"

She waved her wand and Rachel and
Kirsty felt themselves being lifted into
the air. The warm rain sprinkled against
their faces as Mae's fairy magic whisked
them across the world. A few moments
later, they were standing at the entrance
to the nature reserve and Becky was
hurrying towards them.

"There you are, girls!" she called.
"I was beginning to wonder if you'd got
lost! Did you have a good time?"

"Wonderful!" said Kirsty.

"Spectacular!" said Rachel with a beaming smile.

"That's great!" said Becky. "Right, I've got a job for you to do. We've cleared a space for some new trees, so I'd like you to plant the saplings."

Becky showed them where the young trees were lying on the ground beside a number of holes. She told them how to plant each one in its own hole. Just then, her radio crackled and the girls heard a muffled voice.

"It sounds as if I'm needed up at the lake," Becky said. "Is it okay if I leave you to start planting?"

"Of course," replied Kirsty. "We'll come and find you when we've finished."

Becky hurried away, and Rachel picked up one of the saplings. She placed it in a hole, but it started to bend sideways.

"The trunks aren't sturdy enough to stand up by themselves," she said. "What are we going to do?"

As the girls stared at each other, there was a whooshing sound. A little sprinkling of rainbow-coloured fairy dust fell around them, and for a moment they thought they could smell the fresh, wet scent of the bamboo forest. Then they saw a bundle of bamboo poles on the ground between them, tied together with a thin rope made from grass.

"Look, there's a note," said Rachel.

Thank you!
With love from Mae and the pandas

At the bottom of the note were two panda paw prints from Mother Panda and Pan Pan.

"What a lovely present," said Kirsty, sounding puzzled. "But how can bamboo help us?"

"I know!" said Rachel. "Remember how tall the bamboo grew in the forest? I bet the bamboo could help teach the saplings how to stand up straight!"

Eagerly, the girls set to work. Before very long, they had planted all the saplings, using the bamboo poles to support them. Becky came back just as they were finishing the last tree.

"That's fantastic, girls!" she exclaimed. "What a good way to use those bamboo poles, too. Where did you find them?"

"Oh, they were just lying around," said

Rachel with a smile.

"Great work," said Becky. "I've got a little reward for you."

She pulled out a little box, which the girls could see was full of badges. Each badge had a different picture on it, and Becky sorted through them until she found what she was looking for.

"These badges show that you've helped to conserve trees," she said, handing one to each girl.

The badges had a picture of a tree on them. The girls pinned them on, feeling very proud.

"I can't wait to show Mum and Dad," said Kirsty.

Rachel looked at her watch.

"They'll be here to collect us soon," she said. "Wow, today has gone so fast!"

"That's good," said Becky. "I hope you've had fun."

"More fun than we could ever have imagined," Kirsty replied. "I can't wait to see what tomorrow will bring!"

As Becky turned away, the best friends smiled at each other and Rachel gave a wink. "More fairy adventures, I hope!"

**Now it's time for Kirsty and
Rachel to help...**

Kitty the Tiger Fairy

Read on for a sneak peek...

"I can't wait to find out what we'll be doing today!" Rachel Walker exclaimed eagerly as she followed her best friend, Kirsty Tate, through Wild Woods Nature Reserve. "I hope we see lots of different animals."

It was the school summer holidays, and the girls' parents had arranged for them to spend a week as junior rangers at Kirsty's local nature reserve. The reserve was a haven for all kinds of animals like hares, otters and red squirrels.

"We'll have loads of lovely photos to remind us of our time here at Wild

Woods," Kirsty remarked as the girls wound their way through the trees, carrying their backpacks. She stopped to snap a red-and-blue butterfly drinking nectar from a drift of wildflowers and then showed the photo to Rachel.

"It's beautiful," Rachel said admiringly. "Look, Kirsty, there's Becky with the other junior rangers." She pointed to the clearing ahead of them where a group of girls and boys were gathered around the head of the nature reserve. "I bet she's got some interesting jobs for us!"

Read **Kitty the Tiger Fairy** to find out what adventures are in store for Kirsty and Rachel!

Meet the
Baby Animal Rescue
Fairies

Mae the Panda Fairy

Kitty the Tiger Fairy

Mara the Meerkat Fairy

Savannah the Zebra Fairy

Kimberley the Koala Fairy

Rosie the Honey Bear Fairy

Anna the Arctic Fox Fairy

The Baby Animal Rescue Fairies have lost all their magical
items. But luckily, Kirsty and Rachel are there to
save the day and make sure all baby animals
in the world are safe and sound.

www.rainbowmagicbooks.co.uk

Look out for the next sparkly
Rainbow Magic Special!

Robyn the Christmas Party Fairy

Rachel and Kirsty are helping to organise a big Christmas party.
But Jack Frost has stolen Robyn the Christmas Party Fairy's
magical objects! The girls must help Robyn,
before the spirit of Christmas is lost forever...

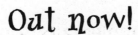

Out now!

Meet the fairies, play games
and get sneak peeks at
the latest books!

There's fairy fun for everyone at

www.rainbowmagicbooks.co.uk

You'll find great activities, competitions, stories and
fairy profiles, and also a special newsletter.

Competition!

The Baby Animal Rescue Fairies have created
a special competition just for you!
In the back of each book in the series there will be
a question for you to answer.
Once you have collected all the books and all
seven answers, go online and enter the competition!

We will put all the correct entries into a draw and select
a winner to receive a special Rainbow Magic Goody Bag,
featuring lots of treats for you and your fairy friends.
The winner will also star in a new Rainbow Magic story!

**Which Fairy is in charge
of birthdays?**

— — — — —

Enter online now at www.rainbowmagicbooks.co.uk

Meet the
Rainbow Fairies

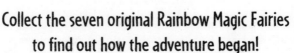

Also available as an ebook

Collect the seven original Rainbow Magic Fairies
to find out how the adventure began!

www.rainbowmagicbooks.co.uk